Halloween Spice

5 MM Stories

D LaMarque

Kelpie Heart Studio

Halloween Spice

ISBN 978-1-0670421-5-8 (paperback)

LOCKED IN A STRAITJACKET

and dommed by my frat brother

A Halloween MM BDSM Erotica

D LaMarque

CHaPTer one

I was minding my own business at the frat house dining table, reading a novel for English class, when Brad sat down opposite me.

"What's your plan for the Halloween party tonight?"

The Psi Phi Sigma house always held a big blowout costume party, but I didn't always go. I tried not to drink too much as it affected my game. So, when Halloween came around, I usually preferred to study. But this year would be different.

"I don't have a plan." That was a lie, I had made a promise to myself to try something new.

Brad leaned his chin on his hand and grinned at me. "Yeah? You got a costume?"

"Not yet."

"Neither. Want to go looking today? Like, what are you doing right now?"

I nodded slowly. "Sure, why not?"

We made our way past the guys already putting up decorations. "You got Andy a costume, yet Brad?" One of the brothers called out.

"We're getting costumes right now!" Brad replied.

The walk to the shops was short, and it gave me a good excuse to check out Brad. He was camp, and annoying, but he was absolutely gorgeous. I'd never been brave enough to say anything about how attracted I was to Brad, always afraid to ruin our friendship. But moments like this were fun.

We walked into the Spirit Halloween and looked over the bags of costumes. There were so many options, but none of them were quite what I wanted.

"I don't know about the quality of this fabric..." Brad rubbed a vampire cape between his fingers and curled his lip.

"Yeah. They don't really have what I wanted," I said.

Brad turned to me, a smile playing over his features. "Oh? You have an idea? What are you looking for?"

"Well." I turned away, pretending to look through the bags so I didn't have to admit this to Brad while looking him in the eyes. "I wanted a straitjacket."

"Okay, why?"

I turned back, biting my lip. I didn't want to admit it was because I'd always wanted to know what it felt like to be bound up in one. For the last few years, I'd had fantasies, urges, watched a lot of bondage porn. This was my excuse to try it out in a safe way, in a way no one would question.

"Uh, you know, I thought I'd do a kind of Joker thing, classic Halloween madman, or serial killer vibe."

Brad nodded slowly. "Well. I know where you could get a good one, none of this shitty quality and plastic buckles."

Relief washed over me, Brad didn't seem to think it was a weird idea. "You do? Lead on then."

I regretted saying that the second I realized Brad was taking me into an adult toy store.

"Why the fuck are we here?" I grabbed Brad and hissed in his ear.

"Because they have high quality costume items that can withstand hard use." Brad shrugged as if he came in all the time. "And I expect whatever we end up wearing at the frat party will be used hard."

I couldn't help but shiver, imagining Brad using me hard. I swallowed that desire down and looked around. I could feel my cheeks blushing as Brad led me inside, but my eye was instantly drawn to the bondage section. There was a whole wall with leather cuffs, whips, crops, and a rack of harnesses and costumes. Black leather, shiny vinyl, shiny silver hardware all called to me. And there, right on the end of the rack, a selection of pristine white canvas straitjackets.

We walked over together. Brad got busy looking through the rack, clicking coat hangers and examining his options.

I took one of the straitjackets down. It was more expensive than I'd expected, but I couldn't quite put it back. It was heavy in my hands, weighty with promise.

The shop assistant came over, a young woman with purple hair and piercings. "Nice pick. It's just your size, too," she said.

"It costs so much." I sounded panicked, I tried to calm myself.

"You're paying for quality with this brand." She tapped the silver buckles. "You see these little loops? The buckles are fully lockable, so you can really feel owned, trapped, you know?" I blushed deeper. The woman looked at Brad and winked. "We sell the padlocks that fit this, if you want to try it."

I carefully pictured the least sexy thing I could imagine; I couldn't get a hard on. Not now. "We're not — we're just frat brothers."

"Sure, sorry." She smiled, unfazed. "But as I was saying this is the real deal. None of that stage magician bullshit you can slip out of. This is inescapable when fastened correctly."

"Fuck," Brad breathed.

I looked at him sharply. Brad turned away and pulled out a sexy nurse dress, all tight white spandex with red details. "Think I could squeeze into this? I want to show off my legs."

The thought of Brad in a tight little dress with a boob window built in was almost too much for me. I had to get out of there.

"Yeah, good. I'll get this." I thrust the jacket at the girl and escaped to the check out. I could take some money out of my savings; it'd be worth it.

I waited outside while Brad fussed with choosing accessories for himself.

This was going to be a wild night.

CHAPTER TWO

That night Brad came into my room before I'd even considered getting ready. He was already dressed. His long, toned legs were on display in red fishnets and shiny heels. The nurse costume hugged his body beautifully and the boob window showed off his hard pecs. He even had the little nurse hat perched in his hair. By all rights he should have looked ridiculous. Instead, he was the hottest thing I'd ever seen.

"You look..." the words died on my tongue. I had no way of telling him how hot he was and still be just a friend. "I know." Brad said. He spun in place, showing off the way the dress hugged his pert, round ass.

He turned back and raised a finger. "Anyway. Since you're my responsibility tonight, I figured I'd help you get suited up."

"Your responsibility?" my eyebrows shot up, suddenly my heart was thudding.

"You're the inmate, I'm the nurse at the asylum." Brad touched himself on the chest and fluttered his eyelashes. "And I do *not* think you can get that jacket done up on your own."

"Well, no. Good point." I closed my laptop on my homework and looked at the jacket. I'd hung it on the wall on its own hanger, pride of place.

"Well, first things first. What are you wearing with it?"

I answered honestly. "I hadn't thought that far."

Brad rolled his eyes. "I should have guessed. I suggest a jock strap, then some relatively loose pants and a tank top."

"Jock strap?" I blinked at him, surprised.

"Yeah. The straps from that jacket are gonna frame your junk. You want to keep it all contained; don't you think?"

I felt my cheeks heat up. "Yeah." I dug out the jockstrap I used for football and a pair of black cargo pants. Brad watched as I stripped off my comfy clothes. "You mind?"

"Not at all." Brad grinned. "I've seen it all before. Remember skinny dipping last summer?"

I didn't reply, because thinking about skinny dipping reminded me of how hot Brad was naked.

I pulled on the jockstrap, adjusting myself until it sat correctly, then put on my tank top and pants.

Brad watched me the entire time. I thought I saw him biting his lip, but I wasn't sure.

"You ready for this?" Brad took the jacket off the hanger.

"Ready."

"Then turn around, prisoner." His order, and the name calling, sent chills through my body, goosebumps and electricity making the hairs on my arms stand up. "I... what?"

"Did I fucking stutter?" Brad took hold of my shoulder and turned me to face him. "Hold out your arms if you know what's good for you."

My mouth was dry. I'd never wanted him more. His authoritative tone was arousing me deeply. I held my arms out to the front.

Brad nodded, mollified. "Good."

He slipped the jacket on me. The canvas was rough on my bare skin, and I was glad I'd worn something to cover my nipples to stop them chafing.

"Turn around, prisoner."

I turned. "You don't have to do the whole bit," I said. If he kept going like this, I wasn't going to be able to hide how horny I was.

"It's Halloween, Andy." Brad pulled the jacket snug onto my shoulders and adjusted it, so it was sitting right. "It's all about getting out of your comfort zone. Playing a part, becoming your darkest fantasy."

I breathed out, suddenly suspecting he knew more than he was letting on. "Fantasy?"

Brad buckled the first strap in the back of the jacket, I felt it pull tight across my chest. "Isn't that why you wanted this jacket?"

"I... yeah, I guess."

"Dirty boy." I could hear the smirk in his voice, it was a reassuringly familiar tone.

"I just..." he couldn't see my face, couldn't see how hard I was blushing. "I don't know, I've always been curious."

"Me, too." Brad cinched another strap tight around my waist. The jacket was slowly constricting, forming itself around my body with the straps, exactly how I'd always imagined it would.

"You, Brad? You're curious about wearing a straitjacket?"

"No." Brad took hold of the topmost straps, the ones that formed a stiff collar around my neck and buckled them snugly. "I've been curious about how fucking needy and wanton you're going to get when you're bound up in a straitjacket."

I forgot how to breathe for a moment. Brad did up the last of the torso straps, then reached between my legs to grab the two hanging straps that would go through my crotch. He brushed my engorged cock with his wrist.

"Mm. So far, so good."

I moaned, I couldn't help it. The jacket felt so good, enclosing me, and Brad's words were absolutely hitting my buttons.

Brad fastened the crotch straps to the back of the jacket, right over my ass cheeks, pulling them tights. They framed the jockstrap perfectly, fixing everything into strict position. I adjusted myself with one sleeved hand.

"Ugh. If we didn't have to make an appearance at this party, I'd have told you to leave your pants off. I know. Next time, I'll prep you first and stuff you up with a butt plug. Then I'll you you're all ready for me to fuck you the entire time you're in the jacket."

"Brad!" I sounded both scandalized and deeply aroused.

Brad paused in tightening each of the straps and gently turned me to face him.

"Andy, since you're being amazingly thick about this, I'll be perfectly clear. I want you. You're hot and funny and clever, and ever since I saw that BDSM tab on your laptop, I've wanted to make you mine. You gave me the perfect opportunity with your costume. Now, are you in?"

My body felt hot all over. My head spun but there was only one possible response. "Yes. Yes, Brad, you're so hot. I want to be yours, so, so badly."

Brad grinned wide. "Thought so. Now, say you're my prisoner and you're at my mercy."

"I'm—" the words were difficult to say, they were so humiliating. "I'm your prisoner. I'm at your mercy."

"That's a good prisoner. But you're not quite at my mercy yet..."

Brad took hold of one the long straps at the ends of my extra-long sleeves and threaded it through the stiff canvas loop on my chest. "I think there's another... yes." He slipped the sleeve through another loop under my armpit."

"You don't — I was going to wear it with the arms loose," I said, helplessly.

Brad snorted. "Not the point of a straitjacket, is it? Besides, you're my prisoner and I want you secure." He threaded the other sleeve through the loops and spun me around. He tugged the sleeves, so my arms were tight across my chest, hugging myself. I felt each tug as he buckled the straps at the ends of the sleeves tight.

"How does that feel, prisoner?"

I swallowed, struggling a little. I could barely move my arms. The jacket was so snug, so perfectly constricting me. I groaned aloud, realizing that my fantasies hadn't prepared me for just how good this would feel.

"I'll take that as a 'yes nurse, it feels good'," Brad teased.

Brad fussed with something, and I felt a tug on the collar of my jacket, followed by a *snick* sound.

"What was that?"

"The nice lady at the shop said this jacket was lockable, so I thought I'd see if she was right. I got a nice handful of locks from her while you were waiting outside. Now, you're padlocked into the jacket, and you *really* can't escape without me."

I whimpered, honest to God whimpered with need.

"Wanton was the right word for you, wasn't it? Bit of a slut, aren't you?"

I whimpered again.

"Want to go down on me prisoner? Show me how eager you are to please your nurse?"

"Yeah," I breathed. I was high on this - endorphins flooded my body. I was bound up, locked in, and I felt freer than ever before.

"Good boy, kneel down for me."

CHAPTER THREE

I hit the floor like Coach had yelled at me. It was lucky my floor was carpeted because I would have done the same regardless. I was so eager to obey him.

Brad walked slowly around me, shark-like. I was quivering with anticipation.

"You look so fucking debauched and all I've done is tie you up."

I swallowed, used to some degree of Brad's taunts. I couldn't deny that I was already way more aroused than I had ever been from vanilla foreplay. I had no response.

Brad stopped directly in front of me.

With one hand he lifted the tight nurse dress and pulled his dick out. He was wearing red panties and fishnets, and now he was stroking himself. "You want this?"

"Yes."

"When you address me, you'll call me Master, and you'll say please and thank you. Understand?"

"Yes, please Master." It probably should have felt wrong, or ridiculous to call Brad 'master' but it was totally natural, and hot as Hell.

"What a good prisoner." With the hand he wasn't jacking off with, he tugged my hair. I moaned, opening my mouth. Brad took advantage of this to push his cock into my mouth.

I licked at the tip of him, swirling around the head with my tongue.

His fingers tightened in my hair. "That's it. Such a good prisoner, I have. You want to be my little sex slave, don't you?"

I relaxed my jaw and leaned in to take him fully into my mouth. I heard him moan and took that as encouragement. I pressed my tongue against his veined hardness. My mouth was swiftly filled with the salt of his precum and I wanted more. I leaned in until he hit the back of my throat and I gagged. I was about to pull back but Brad gripped my hair tight, his other hand on the back of my head, holding me in place. I moaned around him, loving every second.

Gently at first, but becoming rougher, he rocked his hips to fuck my throat.

I looked up at him, through wet eyelashes. He was hitting my gag reflex every time and my eyes were streaming, but I didn't want him to stop. I loved feeling so controlled.

I was also soaking my jockstrap with precum. Being used like this, bound up and treated as a toy? It made my balls tighten. I could probably come just from this, but I didn't let myself.

He groaned and let go of my hair. "Gonna come, if you don't want a mouthful pull back now."

I didn't have to think about it. I leaned further in, ready for him. He grunted, filling my mouth. I swallowed it all down and licked him clean.

"Goddamn, Andy," Brad murmured as he withdrew. He packed himself back into his panties and fishnets. "You're good at that."

I licked my lips. "Thanks, you're hot as fuck in that nurse costume."

Brad smiled, ruffling my hair affectionately. "Now for the fun part."

CHapter Four

"How was that not the fun part?" I wondered.

He grabbed me and pulled me to my feet by one of my biceps. "Should have got you some ankle shackles as well, maybe one of those Hannibal Lector muzzles. That would have been even better."

I swayed at his words, I was so horny my legs were shaking. "Brad—I mean, Master..."

He pulled me in for a hard bruising kiss. I felt his teeth on my lip and then a sharp pain. I tasted blood on my tongue. "Did you just bite me?"

"Oops." Brad grinned mischievously and wiped his mouth. "You're so hot I got carried away. Come on. The others will be wondering where we are, the party started ages ago."

"The others?" I rolled my shoulders, fighting the jacket. "You gonna untie me for the party?"

"Nope." Brad kissed my cheek, a sweet gesture undercut by what he was saying. "You're my prisoner tonight and everyone's going to know it."

I groaned softly in response. He could tell how much I was into this, even if I was kind of complaining.

Brad produced a length of chain and a padlock and made a leash for me by locking the loop of chain around my neck. Then he tugged on it. "Off we go."

I had no choice but to follow him. I was so hard by this point I was grateful for my jockstrap. Above all though, I knew Brad would look after me. He teased me and he was clearly enjoying the power he had over me, but he was also Brad. I'd trust him with my life. If I told him I wanted to stop, seriously told him, I knew he'd stop.

We made it downstairs to the common rooms. The party was ramping up and people from neighboring houses were mingling with our brothers.

Brad leaned in close to whisper in my ear. "What do you think the others will say? Seeing you tied up like this in public?"

My mouth was dry from his words, but in all honesty, the idea of being in public like this thrilled me. I loved the feeling I had of belonging to Brad. The taste of his cum still lingered on my tongue, accented with blood from his bite. It was a secret no one knew but him.

I shrugged and Brad laughed.

"I'll have to feed you your drink, since you can't be trusted to be free."

The other frat brothers laughed when they saw us.

"Ah a couple's costume?"

"Looking good, you two!"

"Brad, your legs look a mile long in that skirt."

"Aw, what'd Andy do? He's usually well-behaved."

"He's a danger to society," Brad said fondly. He grabbed one of the straps on my back and forced me to stop walking.

I gasped, trying my best not to let it turn into a moan. I tried to cover my response. "I was going for like a serial killer thing." My voice was more hoarse than normal, but no one commented on it.

"The jacket looks sturdy." One of the brothers tugged on the jacket, testing the straps, feeling my arm underneath. "Maybe we should keep you in this all the time."

I blushed hard, it was too close to my secret fantasies.

"We could use it on whoever's pissed us off the most each week," someone added.

"Maybe if you don't do your chores, you get put in it." The guys were laughing, joking around.

Brad laughed too, but he slipped his arm around me and pulled me close to his side, away from the wandering hands of our brothers. "You're assuming I'm going to let him out of it."

The guys laughed louder, and a couple of them gave me knowing winks. What did they know? Did they guess that I was into Brad? That I was getting off on them all making fun of me, pointing out my predicament. I *did* want Brad to keep me in the jacket indefinitely, bound at his mercy. The thought was so hot, I leaned harder against Brad without really meaning to.

"Come on, let's get some drinks."

The next hour passed in a haze. Brad held a beer bottle to my lips when I asked for it and kept in almost constant contact with me. I felt cared for. My mind was fuzzy, like I was floating on a cloud of arousal. The pleasure of my fantasy coming true, and the promise of what Brad had promised would happen next combined to make me hot as fuck and blissed out. Brad checked in on me every so often, asking if I was okay, if I needed anything. I was happy though, doing what he said.

Finally, he made excuses to the guys we were talking to and took me upstairs, back to his room.

CHAPTER FIVE

"All right, prisoner. The time has come."

"Please, yes."

Brad grinned at the broken way I'd responded. My voice had cracked, betraying how much I wanted him. "I'm gonna prep you, then fuck you. Any objections?"

I took my head. "Want you so bad, nurse."

"I think I told you to call me Master."

"Master, sorry."

Brad had lost his little hat somewhere downstairs. Now he pulled the dress open, and moved in close to kiss me. I opened my mouth to him and moaned.

I wanted so badly to touch him, to slide my fingers over his toned chest, but the fact that I couldn't made it even hotter.

Brad moved his hands slowly over me, teasing, tugging gently on the straps to remind me how bound up I was. He reached behind to undo the straps around my crotch. I felt the difference in pressure around my balls instantly. I'd adjusted to it, got used to it, the jacket almost felt like a part of me now. His deft hands removed my pants, shoving them down so I could step out of them. Then he gripped my dick through the jockstrap. I cried out, more of a wail than a moan.

I'd been some form of hard for the last few hours, I was aching for release.

"A cock ring next time," Brad murmured, like he was setting himself a mental reminder. He bit down on my earlobe, and I groaned again.

"Or maybe I should get one of those chastity cages, lock your dick up in one of those and then the straitjacket. Plug you up so you're ready for me at any time. You'd really be at my mercy then, wouldn't you?"

I could have come from those words. Brad must have felt me tense because he let go abruptly. "Turn around and bend over the bed. I gotta prep you."

The preparation was interminable. Now we were so close to fucking, I was desperate for it. I've always been a needy bottom, and that was dialed up to a hundred now.

Brad spanked my ass every time I bucked my hips, which made me hotter still.

"Quiet, prisoner. Do I need to gag you too? Can't have you screaming down the house."

"God." A gag sounded like exactly what I needed. "Yes, please Master." I was past being embarrassed now. I had fully adjusted to the role of prisoner, and I wanted anything he was willing to give me.

Brad chuckled darkly and moved away. A second later he pressed a ball gag into my mouth. I was already panting and offered him no resistance. I took it gladly, moaning as he buckled it in the back of my head. I was entirely his.

"Okay, shake your head if you need me to stop. You ready for me? I need to fuck you, like NEED."

I nodded, trying to express approval behind the gag. I didn't care if it hurt when he fucked me.

"Good prisoner." He slicked himself with lube and pushed inside with a groan.

I howled behind the gag as Brad stretched me open. His cock inside me was a burn, hot and sharp and just what I needed. I bucked my hips, unable to stop myself, I was so worked up.

"You're so hot for me, aren't you? If you were a girl you'd be soaking wet, you want it so bad. Didn't know just how wanton you'd get being tied up and gagged for me. Love being helpless, don't you?" His voice broke as he teased me.

Suddenly, he leaned down and bit my neck, worrying at it like a dog, at the same time he wrapped an arm around my chest. "It's too hot, I can't hold back, Andy."

I moaned, rutting against the bed. The slightly changed angle from his holding me had him hitting my sweet spot over and over, and I came suddenly, spilling into my strap, and squeezing Brad as I cried into the gag.

Brad groaned, shoved deep inside, burying himself in me, as he came.

"Fuck," he breathed.

For a moment we just lay like that, locked together, his arm around me, his dick softening in my ass. I closed my eyes and tried to catch my breath. My jaw had started to ache. I could feel the wetness of my drool on my chin leaking onto the bed below me. My bliss had been absolute a moment before, but now reality started to seep back in, I was stimulated in every way and in need of... something.

Brad groaned, pulling out and letting go of me in one movement. He undid the buckle on the back of the gag and tugged it free of my mouth. I moaned, closing my mouth finally and swallowing down some of the drool.

Brad cleaned me with a damp cloth, then eased the jockstrap down my legs and off. He gently cleaned my front too. He left the room briefly, and using my shaking legs, I managed to roll over.

I wasn't at all sure what would happen next, but I knew I wanted to pledge myself to him. To offer to be his prisoner and slave for real.

Brad returned, looking wrecked. The makeup he'd put on had run down his cheeks, and his nurse costume was gone, replaced with a silky bathrobe. He sat beside me on the bed.

"Well," he said.

I licked my lips. "Yeah. That was awesome. But um, are you planning on letting me out of this jacket?"

Brad shook his head, and a rush of warmth shot through me. "You haven't told me to stop, and you know what? You came without my permission. You broke a rule. That's a very bad crime and I think you need to stay restrained as a punishment."

I bit my lip. "Is that so? You never said that was a rule."

"It was implied when you accepted me as your Master. I think I'll chain you to the bed, see how needy you get for me. Maybe if you beg me just right, I'll go down on you. In a few hours. How does that sound, prisoner?"

He was offering so much: to be my Dom, to keep me how I needed to be, and more — to look after me. He committed so much time and energy to me, and I felt truly honored.

"Yes, Master. That sounds like fair treatment."

Brad climbed up to straddle my lap. He kissed me long and slow, romantic, and I knew we'd just sealed our commitment to each other.

GAGGED AND BOUND

BOUND

In public, under my
Halloween costume

A Halloween MM BDSM Erotica

D LaMarque

CHaPTer one

"Think fast!" That was all the warning I had before Cal tackled me.

I'd been minding my own business, washing dishes in the Psi Phi Sigma house kitchen. I managed to not break anything before he had my arm in a vice grip, pressing me against the counter.

I twisted towards him, kicking out with one leg blindly, hoping to trip him. He took the kick with a pained grunt. I pushed my advantage and shoved him to the ground. He still had a hold of my arm, pulling me down with him. We wrestled in silence except for grunts and heavy breathing, until he pinned me, both my arms over my head and his thigh hard between my thighs.

"Got ya."

"Yeah you do." I couldn't look away from his mouth. In the last couple of months our play fights had become more and more charged. I had the wild urge to lean up and kiss him.

Cal leaned further in, like he was considering it too. My heart sped up, was it really going to happen?

The front door slammed and Cal hurriedly climbed off of me. "So. You ready to come Trick or Treating, Rick?"

Every year our fraternity had a big blowout Halloween party, but before that the campus did a Trick or Treat evening. All the Greek houses, a few of the nearby houses and the college library all participated. I didn't usually bother with it, but Cal was weirdly hyped about it this year.

"You gotta come. I just beat you again, you owe me."

He offered me his hand and I took it to pull myself up off the floor. "Sure. I just gotta cut two holes in a sheet then I'm good to go." My lack of inspiration for a costume didn't escape Cal. "You're so predictable."

"What's your costume, then?" I finished up the dishes and drained the sink.

"I got a vintage Ghostbusters costume online."

I turned to him. Was it a coincidence? "Yeah?"

"Mmhm. Maybe I'll catch you for real," he said it slow, raising an eyebrow. I had to look away, think unsexy thoughts. I tried to make a joke and break the tension.

"I don't think I'll fit into one of those little boxes, Cal."

"No, but I have rope in my room and that's one size fits all."

I swallowed. Was he being serious or was this all a joke? "Rope?"

"Yeah. Ricky, I've seen the Instagrams you follow. You like rope a lot, don't you?"

Heat spread across my cheeks and down my neck. "When did you stalk my Instagram?"

"You leave your phone unlocked and just lying around. You should really be careful when you're searching those kinky tags, you never know who might notice."

I covered my face with both hands. "Fuck."

"I mean, unless you'd rather be the one in charge of the ropes, not in them?"

I shook my head. "No."

"That's what I thought." Cal's voice was closer than before. I dropped my hands. "I've also been thinking you let me win our little play fights because you like to be pinned under me."

"Cal..." I swallowed, unable to deny it.

He smiled, reassuring and warm. "If you're not into it, it's no big deal. But if you're up for experimenting then come to my room when you're in your costume and I'll chase you, wrestle you into submission." He smacked his lips, relishing the thought, apparently.

I bit my lip. I didn't need time to think about it. Cal was tall, with gorgeous ochre brown skin and a jawline to die for. I did love being pinned under him. He'd found out about my kinky interests and wanted to play? I was in.

"I want to experiment."

Cal's eyes lit up. "Yeah?"

"But you gotta catch me." I dashed out of the kitchen, laughing, suddenly exhilarated. I heard the thunder of feet behind me. I took the stairs two at a time.

"You little shit!" Cal called, I could tell from his tone he was delighted though. "I'll catch you!"

At the top of the stairs had to dodge around Andy, who was surprised to say the least. I made for my room. Cal was hard on my heels.

"Get back here!"

I had to stop to yank open my bedroom door.

Cal was on me instantly. He wrapped his arms around me, pinning my arms to my sides. "Into my room." He marched me, holding on tight while I struggled ineffectually. He maneuvered me into his room and kicked the door shut behind us. He shoved me onto the bed, where I landed awkwardly.

"Okay, how far are you willing to take this experiment, because I have thoughts."

I breathed out, running a hand through my hair. "You're hot. I trust you, and you — apparently — know what I like, so... pretty far."

Cal's grin was wicked. "I do know what you like. I like it too."

He pinned me on my back, straddling my hips, and kissed me. It was everything I'd hoped it would be — hard and rough, and hungry. He kissed me like he wanted to devour me, and I wanted him to. He stroked one hand down my arms and along my side, possessive and teasing. I arched into his hand.

"I'm gonna wreck you, Ricky."

I moaned into his mouth. "Do it."

"Fuck." Cal pulled back. "Go change into something loose and comfy and bring your damn sheet back here."

He moved off me and I obeyed instantly. I was sporting a half-chub and the thought of loose pants was enticing. I changed into black sweatpants and an oversize T-shirt. Picking up the sheet, I hesitated for a moment. What I was about to do would change things forever. My heart thudded, should I really go through with it?

CHAPTER TWO

I went back to Cal's room with my heart in my mouth. I was practically salivating with anticipation. What would he do? Did he really mean to put me in ropes?

"Ah, so obedient, such a good boy, Ricky." Cal had a tone of approval that I instantly wanted to hear more of. He had been busy while I changed. There was a coil of rope on the bed, along with a couple of other pieces of equipment. "Ricky, we are going to have the best Halloween ever."

I bit my lip. "Yeah. Looks like." "Just checking, you're STI free?"

I nodded. "I've been in a dry spell, I think you know that, and I was tested right after the last guy."

"I was tested last week, I'm all clear. That's good, it means I can fuck you bareback."

I moaned, then tried belatedly to swallow it down. He heard.

"So cute, Ricky." He picked up the rope. "Let's get started. I'm going to bind your arms. This tie is meant to be good for long stretches of time, but you're going to have to tell me if something gets uncomfortable or your fingers go numb, okay?"

I nodded. I was so hard now, blushing like crazy but I couldn't wait to start. "Okay, how do we start? How do you want me?"

Cal grinned. "Naked, kneeling and begging for my cock, ultimately. But for now turn around and put your hands behind your back."

I did as he said, facing the wall, and he moved closer. "Grab hold of your elbows."

The posture forced me to push my chest out a bit, my shoulders back.

He went to work, wrapping the rope multiple times around my wrists and forearms, knotting it, tugging on my arms. Next he wound more rope around my biceps, over my shoulders, and crisscrossing over my chest. It was a shibari harness, I'd seen patterns like this before online.

The ropes were tight but they didn't cut in, it was a pleasant pressure, not painful. The harness felt secure. He fussed over the ropes, checking the knots and making small adjustments here and there.

"I had no idea you knew how to do this." My voice was more moan than normal speaking.

Cal looked up and winked. "I had motivation to learn."

I melted, enjoying the implication that he'd learned just for me. With his ropes tight around my torso and arms, I felt utterly under his control. The thought gave me a headrush.

Finally, he seemed satisfied with his work. He had been moving slowly around me. Suddenly I felt the warmth of his body pressing against me from behind. He played his fingers over my bound chest and rubbed his hardness against my ass. "You look so tempting, Ricky," he murmured. "I tipped my head back to rest on his shoulder, giving in to his care and reveling in it.

"It's so hot, Cal. Touch me?"

"Uh uh." He nipped my neck. "Not until after we've gone trick or treating."

I flushed, imagining going out in public like this, all but helpless, at Cal's whim. My body reacted to it very, very positively.

"But I'm so hard," I whined.

"I know, baby. But I have something for that." He chuckled darkly, letting go of me to pick up a small black silicon ring and grinned. "Cock ring."

"Oh, fuck." I squirmed, testing the ropes. He'd done his job right, I couldn't get free. In fact, I could barely move my arms from the position they were bound in.

"Fuck is right." He popped open my pants, reached inside and stroked my hard dick. "Already so hard aren't you, Ricky? You like the ropes?"

"Yeah." I couldn't deny it. He had the evidence in his hand. I rocked my hips, loving the warm friction of his hand. Just a little more and I might —

He let go.

I whimpered.

"Gotta let you get soft. Next time, this is the first thing I'll put on you."

Next time. I groaned, needy as I've ever been. "Cal..." "Mm. You'd better think unsexy thoughts, or I'll have to get a cup of ice to take care of the situation and I don't think either of us would enjoy that."

He turned away to start changing into his Ghostbusters jumpsuit.

I looked at the ceiling and tried to remember the facts I needed to know for my History class. I breathed slowly, forcing my body to calm down. Thinking of long-dead British kings did the job.

"There you go. Such a good, obedient slut for me."

The next thing I knew my dick was wet with lube and Cal was sliding the stretchy ring up into my pubic hair, settling securely around the root of my dick I groaned, reacting to the pressure. My dick strained against her ring then softened again.

I groaned.

"Good." Cal tucked me back into my underwear and pants, then he draped the sheet over me and very carefully cut eyeholes for me to see through. "You know the beauty of a sheet?" It will hide the ropes. It'll hide almost anything. I could gag you under there and no one would know."

I moaned in response.

"You like that idea? I bet you could still make ghostly moaning sounds behind a gag. You really are thirsty. Now, before I gag you..." he pulled the sheet off. "What names are you okay with me calling you?"

I swallowed as Cal picked up a roll of duct tape. He was really going to do it. "Um. I don't mind slut. You could call me boy too, and baby was good."

Cal kissed me hard. I groaned, opening my mouth and letting him control it. He lashed his tongue against mine then pulled back.

"Good boy. Now, no more talking. If you've had enough or need a break, kick my ankle, got it? That will be our safeword for while you're gagged."

I swallowed, heart pounding. I didn't think I'd need a safeword but it was reassuring to know he'd considered it. "Yeah. Got it."

He pulled a length of duct tape out from the roll. It made an incredible sound, the promise of something. He placed the strip of tape over my mouth, smoothing it down gently with his fingertips. He tore another strip of tape off and smoothed it over the first, then added a third strip that went a bit lower, securing the tape over my lower lips by extending the gag onto my chin.

"Some time," Cal murmured as he worked. "I want to only use tape on you. Tie your hands behind your back with it, then make you into an entire duct tape mummy. Just leave your dick and balls out in the front, and your ass in back, so all you can do is wriggle and take it as I fuck you over and over, leave you like that for hours, and use you..." He hummed, clearly relishing the idea. I nodded, slightly, a moan muffled by the tape. "You like that idea, huh? Maybe tomorrow, then."

I leaned in, wanting something — a kiss, or some kind of touch. Reassurance maybe.

Cal seemed to understand and wrapped his arms around me, kissing the tape over my mouth. I could feel it, less intense than lip to lip, but the pressure was there. Knowing I couldn't kiss back, my mouth was sealed shut, made it so hot I bucked my hips against him. "Such a good boy for me We're going to have so much fun together, Ricky." He grabbed the sheet and threw it over me, adjusting it so the holes were over my eyes and I could see out.

"Hmm. I don't want this slipping around, how can I? I know."

He produced a length of chain from the drawer under his bed and wrapped it loosely around my neck, fastening it with a heavy padlock. The chain had a long tail that he took hold of. "Now I have a leash for you, too. No running away now, this could bruise if I have to yank you back with it. But you'll be a good boy for me, won't you?"

I whimpered, nodding.

He grinned. "Let's go trick or treating.

CHapTer THree

The other brothers laughed when they saw us dressed up. Cal had got into character, telling them I was a troublesome ghost he'd had to chase up and down to capture. I attempted a spooky moan and it sounded pretty good behind the gag. They all snapped pictures of us.

Knowing that they were all taking photos of me bound up and gagged under my costume was a hot secret, one only Cal and I knew. It was a powerful feeling, knowing something like that, a shared thing for just us two. The others would all have photos but they didn't know the whole story.

Cal led the way out of the house, my chain in one hand and a plastic bucket in the other. The various houses had decorated for the event and there were lots of others out in costume to collect candy. I saw angels, demons, a cop and prisoner — the prisoner was cuffed, which made me feel a kinship to him). We walked past another sheet ghost, who raised their hand to wave. I nodded back, hoping they wouldn't think me rude for not waving back, but I literally couldn't.

I was glad Cal had put the cock ring on me because every time I got reminders of my predicament, I was aroused all over again.

Cal was having a blast. He led me up the path to a sorority house. The girls there squealed and laughed, insisting on posing with us for multiple photos.

These photos would probably end up on social media. No one knew I was tied up of course, but everyone could clearly see Cal had me on a chain leash. Those pictures would be everywhere, and given everyone knew we were friends they'd probably tag me in them. Photos of me online, chained up...

I was aroused as fuck, and suddenly eager to get back home so I could get the cock ring off, so Cal could fuck me.

But at the same time, I wanted to prolong it. I wanted this anticipation, this torture of being paraded around, bound and horny, to continue. I was bright red, I could feel it, glad to be hidden under the sheet so people couldn't tell how much I was getting off on it.

Cal was in no hurry. He took us up the road, stopping at each house and getting as much candy as he could.

Being tied up on a hot man's leash in public was intoxicating. I started to work my jaw, trying to open my mouth just so I could feel the tape sealing it shut all over again. Teasing myself with it. Every little tug on the chain was another thrill, knowing I had no choice but to go where he wanted. I was sweating with need.

After one house he slipped his arm around me and kissed the side of my head. "Isn't this fun, Ricky-boy? I shoulda put a ring on myself. Every time I think of you tied up under there, I get so hard. You have no idea how hot you look with a tape gag. Can't wait to get you on your front and fuck you hard."

I whimpered, leaning against him. I'd never whimpered before so much in my life. Maybe next Halloween I could be a dog, and he'd keep me on a leash again.

I was already thinking about next year?

I wanted it. I wanted more. I wanted to be his bound-up fucktoy forever.

"Just one more house than we'll call it." He took us up to one more house — we'd be missing half a dozen if we went home after this. I was impatient, bouncing on the balls of my feet.

Then he tugged me by the chain off the main street and down a dark alley between two frat houses.

"Can't wait, baby. Need you now."

I nodded enthusiastically. I hadn't imagined this was on the cards— did he really mean to fuck me in public?

He found a spot behind some bushes, hidden from the street, and the nearest windows were curtained so no one would be watching. He turned me to face the brick wall with his hands firm on my shoulders. He yanked my pants down and hiked the sheet up around my shoulders.

"You want this, Ricky?"

I nodded furiously, saying 'yes, yes' behind the gag but of course, it was muffled.

"Fuck."

There was cold lube on my hole suddenly. For whatever reason he'd brought it with him. Maybe he'd anticipated his own impatience?

He started to prep me roughly, his fingers moving fast and urgent, using way too much lube.

"Hah. It's like ectoplasm," he joked.

I was beyond jokes. I needed him. I spread my legs wide as they could go with my pants around my ankles and arched my back, encouraging him to work faster, showing him how much I needed it.

"Soon, baby." He mouthed over the sheet at my neck, grinding himself against his own hand where he was stretching me open. It was too much, I was gone, eyes closed I used the wall to hold me up and moaned wantonly behind the gag.

"Ready?"

I nodded, unable to tell him to go faster but trying all the same. Hearing me try to talk behind the gag seemed to spur him on. His hard cock pushed against the tight ring of muscle then he was inside, stretching me with a sting that I relished.

I moaned my need, trying to beg for more just to see if it would make him go faster.

He wrapped an arm tight around me, his hand on my chest, and used that for leverage, fucking into me hard and fast.

It hurt, but in the best possible way.

I wanted it to hurt more. There had been so much build-up, so much kinky foreplay, extended time in the ropes where people might see, I wanted him to wreck me. I'd have told him all this if I could have.

Cal seemed to know. He whispered filthy things in my ear as he took me. "Fuck, I can't last. I'm gonna come. You wanna come? I bet you do, baby. Such a kinky slut for me, probably would have come already if I hadn't put that ring on you. Even need your dick tied up don't you? Need to be controlled so bad."

I moaned, bucking back against him with wild abandon.

He reached in front and slid the ring off. The speed with which I got hard made me light-headed.

"Want to feel it when you come. Come for me, slut."

I came instantly, unable to do anything but obey him. I bucked and moaned, shuddering bodily.

He moaned in my ear, thrusting so hard my chest slammed into the wall of the house, gasping as he filled me.

"That's just the first of the night, baby."

CHAPTER FOUR

I was wrecked, just how I'd wanted, but Cal wasn't done with me. He didn't untie me or take off the gag. He pulled out, and I felt something cold and hard pressing against my gaping hole. He teased me with it, pushing it into place after a few thrusts, then patted it fondly.

"Mine," he said, soft but determined.

I shuddered. I could feel his cum inside me, held in by the plug, but more than that, the promise of more was doing things to me. What else would the night hold?

He pulled my underwear and pants back into place.

"I'll clean you up properly later, when I'm done with you. But I think you probably quite like the thought of being used and put away wet, don't you?"

I couldn't deny it, not when my body was trembling from his words.

He set my sheet back into place and fixed himself up. I closed my eyes, floating on the intensity of the orgasm and the feeling of being controlled, being his.

I felt a tug on the chain and pulled myself back to reality with a groan.

We walked back to the house. I had to walk a little more cautiously, not used to the feeling of being plugged up yet. Cal was patient, chatting to me about nothing much as we walked, pointing out people's costumes and the kinds of candy he'd scored for us.

I appreciated his attention. I was in danger of floating away on a bliss bubble and tripping over my own feet.

Finally, finally, we were back at our house and Cal guided me to lead the way up the stairs. I could barely manage the stairs, knees shaking and plug never quite sitting so I could forget it.

Once we were in his room, he locked the door and shoved me onto the bed. I landed hard, overstimulated and moaning. He pulled off my shoes, socks and pants.

I jolted at a sudden sharp pain, he was biting my thigh, sucking hard to create a hickey into the sensitive skin there. Behind the gag I keened — needing more but loving the tease as well.

He yanked my underwear off and stroked my hard dick. "Fuck, baby, you're hard again? You need me, huh? Well, you'll have to wait."

He pulled back and rolled me onto my side.

I heard the *click* of the lock being undone and the chain slipped from around my neck. Next he pulled the sheet free and tossed it aside. "Can you sit up?"

I did my best, but he had to help me. I whimpered as he pulled me upright and the plug in my ass jostled.

Without warning he pulled the duct tape off my face.

I cried out. It stung but my aroused, overstimulated body loved it. It took the pain and added it to the arousal.

"Fuck," I moaned. My voice sounded strained, husky, deeply aroused. In the back of my head I thought I could work one of those phone sex lines with a voice like that.

"How are you doing, baby boy?" Cal smoothed my damp hair back from my forehead. It was a gentle, affectionate gesture that made my heart swell.

"Don't untie me," I said, breathless, suddenly afraid it was all over, despite what he'd said earlier.

Cal's eyebrows shot up and he laughed, kissing me with force. "You want to stay mine?"

"Yeah." I swallowed.

He grabbed a water bottle and held it to my lips. "Drink up."

I drank a third of it in two gulps.

I licked my lips, which felt weird after the glue from the tape. I had to express at least a little of what I'd been feeling. "Cal, I've never felt like this. I love it. I love being yours, your slut, your baby boy. I just... please keep me?"

Cal cupped my cheek. "It's my pleasure baby. I've wanted you for so long and I have so many ideas. If you like, you could just move into my room? Be my live-in sub?"

I nodded, turning my head to kiss his palm. "Want it so bad."

He wrapped his arms around me and pulled me close. "Then you're mine, baby. I'll keep you, I'll look after you."

I closed my eyes, pressing into him, feeling owned and treasured. The bliss only increased at his words. The future held so much fun and fulfillment, I couldn't wait for more.

MUZZLED

In public by my fraternity brother

A Halloween MM BDSM Erotica

D LaMarque

CHAPTER ONE

My phone buzzed, waking me up from the nap I took after my afternoon classes. A message from Leaf — my sometimes fuckbuddy. Honestly, he was the best top I'd ever been with.

Leaf: what are you doing for Halloween?

Joe: Haven't thought about it. You wanna hang out?

Leaf: oh yeah. I'm getting you a costume as we speak and we're doing the campus trick or treat night

I hadn't even registered that it was Halloween. I groaned — a bunch of excited college students drinking and gorging on candy sounded like a headache. I lived off-campus to avoid those situations.

Joe: I'd rather just bang

Leaf: you'll get that if you dress up with me. Please? It'll be fun. I'll make it fun.

He texted again with a handcuffs emoji and I had to adjust myself, suddenly a lot more interested. We'd played around a little bit with bondage and power exchange and I was low-key addicted to it.

Joe: okay
Leaf: come by the house at 6, k? I'll get you dressed up

I thumbsed up his text and went to shower. I didn't jack off, although I wanted to. Instead I used the shower time to tease myself open and prep for later. I liked no having to wait around when we were getting hot and heavy. Once I was out of the shower I lubed a plug and gently pushed it inside. There. He'd love that, and maybe I'd have more fun trick or treating, feeling it while we walked.

I grabbed my overnight things and walked over the Psi Phi Sigma House. They always had a big Halloween party, but it started later in the evening. All the Greek houses participated in Trick or Treat. Everyone would dress up and go house to house for candy or jello shots. Just a bit of fun, mostly for freshmen. I wasn't sure why Leaf wanted to do it so much, but if he was fucking me after with handcuffs then I'd play along.

The house door was open so I walked in and knocked on Leaf's closed door.

"Come in!"

My heart thudded when I saw Leaf's costume. He was dressed as a badass monster hunter with black leather pants, a gray henley, a long leather coat and a big cross around his neck. There was even a shoulder holster under his coat.

"Here's your costume, Joe." He pointed to a pair of torn up jean shorts, a white tank top and a plaid shirt with the sleeves ripped off.

There was a fancy looking werewolf mask beside the pile, I picked it up and got the distinct smell of leather.

"I'm a werewolf?"

"And I'm the monster hunter who caught you." He grinned, sparing a moment from fixing his hair to kiss my cheek. "Go ahead and get changed, but uh, put this on too." He picked up a silicon cockring from his chest of drawers and handed it to me.

I looked at it, bemused. "You serious?"

"Deadly."

I stripped, grabbed some lube and slipped the cockring on, careful to keep my ass facing away from Leaf so he wouldn't see the plug. I slipped it on with a grunt. "Happy?"

"Mm, looks good, babe."

I pulled my underwear back on, then the shorts, they were on the tight side, and there was a big tear in the ass. If I'd left my underwear off my ass would be hanging out. I felt kind of slutty wearing them, which wasn't a bad feeling at all. I added the tank top and shirt and took a look at myself in the mirror.

I looked like someone's lumberjack wet dream, but at least the shirt showed off my biceps.

"Boots too."

I hadn't noticed but he'd got me a new pair of Timberlands too. Leaf was rich, and he often did stuff like this — bought me gifts, always something useful and highly priced.

"Thanks, man, these are great." I sat to put them on.

"Don't mention it, I wanted you to look the part."

He picked something up and came to stand beside me, I turned towards him. He had the werewolf mask, and something else. "This mask isn't just any werewolf mask. It's a custom leather hood, and it's got two parts to it. There's the wolf hood and a muzzle. How do you feel about being muzzled?"

CHapter TWO

"Muzzled?" When he'd said Trick or Treat I hadn't imagined bondage would be part of it. It was hot as fuck. I sat down on the bed, slightly overwhelmed. "I don't know."

"Yeah. Muzzled, it has a built-in collar as well. Fine quality leather, made custom just for you."

"I... I'm interested, how does it work?"

Leaf moved closer, smiling. "How about I show you, and if you hate it, I'll take it off again?"

I breathed out, considering. It was hot. But I wasn't entirely sure I wanted to basically be gagged.

Leaf nudged my knees apart and moved into press against me.

I touched his thighs and squeezed his ass. "I love you in leather." My voice came out a low growl, rough with arousal.

"I think you'll love being in leather too, puppy."

He showed me the leather muzzle. It looked like it was made of leather straps and buckles and little else. It smelled divine.

I swallowed hard, what was I getting myself into? And why did it arouse me so much? I trusted Leaf, so it wasn't like I was going to be in danger. He'd look after me.

I nodded. "Yeah, do it."

The muzzle fitted all the way around my head.

There was a large leather chin piece in front, two straps came up around my nose and connected to a thick strap that went from my forehead to the base of my skull. A collar piece fit around my neck.

Leaf climbed onto the bed and settled behind me to line up the straps. "Hold still, puppy. If it's too tight just say."

He tugged the collar piece tight first, buckling it around my neck. It was thick and heavy, the kind of collar you'd put on a big dog. I felt my skin turn to goosebumps. I was already enjoying this and he'd only fastened one buckle.

He tugged the top straps first, securing the muzzle in place above my ears.

Next he did the straps that secured the chin piece. I could feel it tighten around my face. It was strange but good — a new sensation but something my body was into. I was hardening, my breath coming quicker. He worked slowly and methodically, fastening the straps loosely to start with, then tightening them. The chin piece was pulled tight against my mouth and jaw so it sat snug and secure.

I closed my eyes, it felt incredible. My body felt at peace all of a sudden.

"How's it feel, puppy?"

I nodded and gave him a thumbs up.

"Good, because it looks hot as fuck." He pulled me close with a finger hooked in the collar and kissed the leather of the muzzle.

I moaned, wanting to reciprocate but unable to.

"Now, the werewolf hood fits over the top, you like this? Should I leave the muzzle on?"

I swallowed. He was giving me an out, but I didn't really want it. I liked the way the muzzle and collar made me feel. I nodded.

Leaf grinned. "Good boy. I'll put the mask on now, if it's too much just tap my arm, okay?"

I nodded again. It seemed my communication for the evening would be nodding, shaking my head or moaning predominantly.

Wherever he'd got this muzzle it was clearly well made. It was secure, even knowing how it went on I'd have trouble with the buckles at the back of my head. But it was comfortable as well.

He picked up the werewolf hood and slipped it on my head. It fit perfectly over the muzzle.

My vision was restricted, blinkered by the relatively small eyeholes on either side of the protruding leather snout.

I took a deep breath and found there was no issue. Most of the snout was open around the mouth so breathing wasn't restricted.

The hood had more buckles in the back, I could feel them sit in between the straps and buckles from the muzzle. Leaf tightened them up to a secure but comfortable level.

I was enclosed, masked and muzzled. My hearing was muffled from the leather. I felt more submissive with these pieces on than I'd experienced previously. The muzzle brought something new out in me, I felt incredibly calm, at peace, ready and willing to obey Leaf.

I nuzzled back into Leaf, trying to convey how happy I was, how much the muzzle was doing for me.

"Aw, what a cute puppy." He slipped his arm around me and squeezed. "Okay, one last touch and then we can go."

He clipped a chain leash to my collar and added another length of chain to his belt. "Feeling good?"

I nodded.

"Let's go knock 'em dead." He handed me a plastic bucket in the form of a pumpkin and took one for himself, practically skipping as he lead me out on a leash.

He was serious, we were really going to collect candy like this. I was thankful for the cockring because without it I'd be bursting out of my shorts.

CHAPTER THREE

Outside, the streets were crowded with people in all manner of costumes. My vision was restricted — no peripheral vision — so I had to turn my whole head if I wanted to see what was happening. I saw out Frat brother Cal dressed as a Ghostbuster, and someone alongside him dressed as a sheet ghost. There were two pirates running down the road, one chasing the other, and lots of sorority girls.

I double-taked at one pair of girls, who were dressed as Batgirl and Poison Ivy — Batgirl was wrapped in Ivy's vines. I couldn't tell for sure with my eyesight restricted and their make up but I thought they might be Kappa Beta Nu girls, from the sister sorority to Leaf's frat. I wondered if they were doing something similar to what Leaf and I were... I imagined how hot it'd be to be walked around tied up and not just muzzled, and wished briefly that he'd chained up my arms as well — but I was content with being muzzled. I felt entirely owned, already.

Leaf waved at people, calling out to those he knew, and tugged on my leash, bringing me up the path to the first house for candy.

"Cool mask, bro!" someone said.

I responded with my best growl, a guttural sound that didn't require me to open my mouth. The guy laughed.

"Don't hurt me!"

I felt a sharp yank on my collar and beside me Leaf commanded, "down boy!"

I took a step back, the way he was tugging — my libido loving the roleplay aspect, which was something of a surprise. I'm usually a pretty straightforward guy and don't go in for make believe, but this was amazing.

Leaf chuckled and slapped my ass as we walked away. I made a strangled noise.

He knew I liked to be spanked, he was riling me up on purpose. I loved it.

We walked up and down the road, collecting candy, although my mind wasn't on what types of candy I was getting at all. It was on how I felt like Leaf's possession — his toy or his captive, or both — and how much I was getting off on it.

As we were waiting in line for candy at a particularly busy sorority house, he pressed tight against my back, rubbing his hardness against my ass. "How does it feel, puppy? Being on my chain, muzzled in front of everyone? I think you like it."

I leaned back on him, reaching with one hand to grip his hip and encourage me to dry hump me, to fuck the plug in my ass deeper. I didn't care who could see, I just wanted more of him.

"Such a needy puppy, aren't you? You want everyone to know you're mine. I should have put a name tag on this collar so everyone would know Joe is the one under the mask, that you're the one I'm leading about."

I moaned. He knew me too well. I was getting off on the knowledge people were seeing me chained to him, in a leather collar. I wanted more, wanted him to tie me to a tree and fuck me with everyone watching. It wasn't a good idea — campus security would certainly have something to say about it — but it was so hot I couldn't help but want it.

Leaf rolled his hips against me then pulled away, out of my grasp. "I should make you crawl on your hands and knees." He bit my shoulder in the crook of my neck and I groaned.

With a sharp tug on the collar, he pulled us away from the line and back onto the main drag. "Home now. I can't wait any more, I like being your dom in public way too much.'"

I was glad to hear it, and followed as close as I could. He kept a tight hold on my leash all the way back to his frat house.

Inside he made me climb the stairs first, his hand on my ass, teasing his fingers through the tears in the shorts. I was fully hard by this point, barely held in by the short shorts. I went straight for his room, panting and sweating.

He locked his door and pushed me face first against it. I felt a tug at the back of my head and a moment later he lifted the hood off me.

I blinked, the room light seemed brighter without the mask.

I was still muzzled, and he made no move to take that off. Instead, his hands snaked around me, lifting my tank top up to caress my abs, then teasing down, undoing the shorts and stroking me.

I moaned his name behind the muzzle and he bucked his hips hard up against me. "I'm gonna strip you, chain you to the bed and fuck you so hard you won't be able to walk tomorrow," he growled in my ear. I whimpered my response, unable to do anything else.

He got to work and I moved when he needed me to. Soon I was standing naked except for my muzzle.

"What's this, puppy?" He tapped the base of the plug and I bucked my hips, whining again. "You got yourself all ready for me? You been teasing yourself with this all evening? Keeping it from me?"

He took hold of my bicep and yanked me towards the bed, I stumbled, half-drunk on arousal.

He shoved me to my knees at the head of the bed. "Grip the headboard, puppy."

I did as he said. He pulled out some sturdy looking metal shackles. They were shiny, obviously new, but they resembled something from a medieval dungeon. My mouth went dry, seeing them, knowing they were for me.

He'd really gone to a lot of trouble and expense for this evening... surely it meant he wanted to do this more often. I whimpered, wanting it so bad it hurt.

CHaPTer Four

Leaf shackled me to the head of his bed, winding the chains through the slats of the headboard so I was held tight. The shackles closed with a click but he produced keys and locked them while I watched. I realized how incredibly secure they were, how utterly at his mercy I was. My dick was leaking with need, achingly hard.

He stepped back, looking at me on my knees, gripping the bed, muzzled, chained and plugged. I turned to look at him, groaning to see he was stripping, visibly hard for me.

"I wanna take some pictures, is that okay? I want to remember how hot you look like this."

I nodded my consent, I wanted to see the pictures later, I was sure I could beat off to them again and again, remembering this moment. I arched my back, sticking my ass up as he snapped away on his phone.

Finally, satisfied, he tossed it aside and grabbed the lube. Wasting no time now he moved behind me. "Such a good little puppy, getting yourself ready for me. You'll get a reward for that. Next time I'll get you a puppy tail plug, how about that?"

I whimpered, ridiculously into the idea, and also the promise of a next time. I wanted this kind of treatment all the time.

Leaf tugged at the plug, withdrawing it quickly so I yelped.

He pushed inside me before I could miss the sensation of being stuffed full. His cock stretched me even more than the plug had, a familiar sensation that I loved more every time.

Behind the muzzle, I thanked him, I praised God, I swore, overwhelmed. So much had been building up to this. All evening I'd been anticipating him, teasing myself with the plug, aching against the cock ring. Now that it was happening it was almost too much for me.

I gripped the headboard, my hands white-knuckled.

"You feel so good, so glad I caught you, werewolf," Leaf's voice was strained, betraying his need. He rocked his hips and tugged on the collar. For a moment the leather pressed against my windpipe and I could feel myself squeezing around him.

He groaned, his thrusting becoming more urgent, shoving deep inside me. "You like that, don't you? Being choked while I fuck you?"

I could barely hold myself up any more. My knees shook, and my thighs ached, every part of my body begging for release. I was gasping behind the muzzle, overwhelmed with it all.

Leaf yanked on the leash again and I crumpled forward, pressing my chest against the headboard and my own fists. I tried my best to beg him, but it came out as only needy noises.

He raked his nails down my back. I arched, howling with need.

"That's it, howl for me, wolf."

Leaf's hand wound around front to remove the cockring. My dick was throbbing. He fisted me, his hand working like a piston.

"Come for me, I'm so close, I want to feel you first."

My whole body reacted, I had no idea I could hold back my own orgasm so well but now that I had permission I let loose. I howled again, need, stimulation and release all fuelling the sound.

"Joe, fuck!" Leaf cried out, still pumping my softening dick in his hand as he shoved deep inside me and came.

CHAPTER FIVE

I was a panting mess, barely propped up by the headboard.

Leaf withdrew slowly, grabbing a towel to mop us up, then he carefully unlocked the shackles.

I collapsed onto the pillows, falling sideways.

With infinite care he tugged the buckles loose on the back of the muzzle and with careful, gentle hands he pulled the collar and muzzle free from me.

"You've been such a good puppy for me, Joey."

I smacked my lips and took in a deep breath. I'd been able to breathe fine all night but there was nothing like a big mouthful of air.

"How are you doing?" Leaf rubbed his hand down my spine.

I wanted to reply but I was past words for the moment. I nodded instead, grabbed one of his hands and pulled him on top of me.

"Ah, I got it." He wrapped himself around me, holding me tight. In the absence of the muzzle, it was the enclosed feeling I needed, the sensation of being small, being in his control.

Slowly my mind cleared and I relaxed into his embrace. My muscles had been tense since he unchained me, but now I turned to mush.

"Good, was it then, pup?" he murmured softly.

"Yes." My voice was rough, hoarse, all that howling. "Very good."

"I liked it too."

I shuffled, as much as I could within his arms, to look him in the eyes. His dreamy eyes were full of affection and my heart thudded.

"Let's do that again. A lot."

"Yeah?" Leaf beamed. "I'd love to. You want to be my submissive for real? Only sleep with me? Do as I say? I could move into your apartment or you could move here, and we could really make it work. For the foreseeable future?"

"Forever, yeah." I leaned up to kiss him gently, pouring all my satisfaction and desire for him into it. "Forever sounds good." Leaf squeezed me tight, then reached up to boop my nose. "It's a deal."

SHACKLED

in public at Halloween

A Halloween MM BDSM Erotica

D LaMarque

CHAPTER ONE

"You lose."

I looked up, panting, from my spot on the ground where I'd just tried, and failed, to beat Seth's record of most pushups in one minute. I collapsed onto my front.

Seth beamed at me, enjoying every second of my failure.

Just what possessed me to challenge him to a pushup contest, I had no idea, but there was no denying my defeat. He'd done a full ten more than I had.

Well, I knew *why* I'd provoked him. Seth was gorgeous, tall, muscular, and older. He'd been Psi Phi Kappa for two years already and I was freshly approved at age twenty. I had the biggest crush on him, and I didn't know how to get his attention, how to interact, if it wasn't annoying him. I liked to get a rise out of him, even if it was only to have his attention on me for a few minutes.

He offered me a hand up, and I took it, scowling.

"Well, Billy, you lost, so here's your costume."

I took the offered Halloween costume, new in a plastic bag, and stowed it under my arm. "Fine."

"Get changed, then it's Trick or Treat time."

We went to our respective rooms. The wager had been to choose the opponent's Halloween costume, our frat's party started in a few hours but the street was given over to Trick or Treat until then.

He must have been certain he'd win this competition because he'd had this costume ready to go. I'd challenged him this morning, so I guess he'd gone to the shop since then, but still... cocky.

He'd chosen a boring option for me, a Halloween staple. A prison uniform — basically black and white striped pajamas. Well, at least they'd be comfortable. I pulled it on over my boxers, fixed my hair and made my way downstairs.

I hesitated on the stairs, trying to stop my heart pounding. Seth was dressed like a hot cop stripper. Real Magic Mike stuff with shorts so tight they looked painted on, a blue shirt hanging open to show off his perfect pecs and six-pack. He had a hat, dark glasses and a utility belt with a nightstick and a few pairs of handcuffs hanging from it. I immediately wondered what he was planning to do with those handcuffs, imagining some truly X rated scenarios, but shook it off when he looked over at me.

"There's the inmate, looking good Billy!"

One of the other frat brothers looked over and grinned.

I did a slow turn at the bottom of the stairs, pretending I was a model on a catwalk. I got a few laughs.

"Ah, looks like you're in trouble now, Billy. Seth doesn't play around."

"Yeah," I said. "I'm so intimidated." I rolled my eyes.

Seth grabbed my arm and pulled me in against him. Let's get a selfie."

The abrupt proximity to him had me catch my breath. I did my usual awkward finger guns at the camera. Anything to distract myself from how good Seth smelled — a blend of sweat, pine and fresh linen. I wanted to lick his chest. His arm was so firm and warm around his shoulders.

"Nerd," he teased.

"You're the one dressed as a police officer, what's with that?"

Seth quickly and smoothly moved his arm from around my shoulders to put me into a headlock. "Careful what you call me, scum, I'll throw you in solitary if you're not well-behaved."

I sputtered, struggling to break his hold. He tightened his grip and I struggled to breath under the crush of his muscles. I low-key was getting off on it. He could control me physically, so easily. I wasn't that small a guy, but Seth was just... Captain America built.

I tapped his arm, and he let me go, I took a huge breath and tried my absolute best to pretend the flush was from lack of oxygen, not arousal.

I swallowed. "I'm not very good at behaving." I ran a hand through my hair, trying to play it off.

"That's why I got the matching costumes, so I can keep you in line, discipline you if you need it."

He was making it hard to pretend I wasn't turned on. I was immediately imagining him spanking me, which wasn't something I usually found arousing but Seth was the exception, I guess.

Looking at his face, it was near-impossible to tell what Seth was thinking. His sunglasses hid his eyes and eyebrows. It was impossible to tell if he was flirting, or just having fun with his costume. If he was flirting, I was going to provoke more, I would definitely enjoy more flirting.

"What you gonna do, big guy?" I let my voice drop low, leaning into my natural Georgia drawl. "Gonna throw me over your lap and spank me?"

Seath picked up a beer and sipped it, making me wait for an answer. If he was flirting, he was exceptionally good at the tease.

"Usually, cops throw prisoners in jail but if you'd rather be spanked, that's good to know. Thanks, Billy."

CHAPTER TWO

I was sure he'd see my blush from that one — calling my bluff, so I grabbed his beer off him and took a swig.

He smacked his lips. "Taking property from an officer? Underage drinking? That's strike one, Bill."

I scoffed. My blood was up, and I desperately wanted, no, needed, to see how far he was going to take this. I leaned into sarcasm. "Oooh, a strike system, I'm *so* afraid."

Seth grinned and tapped one of the pairs of cuffs on his belt. "Just keep talking, smart-ass. You'll feel the full force of the law."

I grabbed a handful of candy out of a nearby bowl and stuffed it in my mouth. I had to stop myself making a filthy joke about 'full force' somehow. As I chewed, I could feel the weight of his gaze on me, and I liked it. I loved it. Knowing I had his full attention was as addictive as any drug.

"Just begging for it, aren't you?" he said.

It took a moment for me to swallow the candy but now I was relatively sure that yeah, he was flirting, he knew what he was saying. Hell, he'd picked out these costumes for us to wear, which was usually a couples thing, right?

I looked him over and grabbed the nightstick off his belt. "Begging for what? For you to use your big hard stick on me?"

Seth growled softly and pushed himself off the wall to tower over me. My dick responded instantly. I knew he wouldn't actually hurt me — he'd let me out of the headlock when I'd tapped for mercy after all — but the threat of him was thrilling.

"Give that back." He held out a hand. "Taking it is strike two, not returning it is strike three."

I twirled the stick in my hand and backed away, wanting him to chase me, to throw me down, then to fuck me. I wondered how far he'd go. "No."

"You little…"

I grinned and turned tail, heart thudding in my ears as I ran through the frat house. Dodging past people in various costumes, and the guys decorating for the party later.

I could hear Seth's footsteps, close behind, swearing as he dodged and pursued.

He caught me in the front entranceway, grabbed my arm and slammed me against the wall face first.

I gasped, hadn't expected the roughness but I couldn't deny that I liked it.

"Spread your legs." He twisted my arm behind my back, and I swallowed a groan.

"Fuck you." I felt high, intoxicated by his attention and the brutal way he was acting. I tried to break his hold on me, struggling and squirming. There was no chance. Seth's grip was as strong as steel.

"You're going to be the one getting fucked if you're not careful."

He used his free hand to pat me down, or rather, caress my waist, slide his hand over my abs and pinch my ass.

My body responded to the attention, and I bucked my hips. "Don't threaten me with a good time, officer."

"Cocky little shit," Seth growled.

Something hard and cold clicked shut around my wrist.

He turned me so my back was to the wall and grabbed my other arm, cuffing it to the first.

"There, now you won't be able to get into any more trouble."

I moaned, tugging against the cuffs, then caught myself and bit my tongue. No use, Seth had heard it, how could he not when he was all but pinning me against the wall.

"Kinky little fuck, you like that? You do, don't you? Good news. I have more where that came from." He slipped a chain around my waist and locked it to the cuffs with a padlock.

He spun me back to face the wall and kicked my legs apart. I was pressed against the plaster, moaning as he ground himself against me. "You like that?"

I could feel he was half-hard, and I reveled in it. He was getting off on doing this to me. I had his attention for sure.

"Answer my question."

There was no way I could deny it. "Yeah."

The doorbell rang and Seth let go of me to hand out candy to some guys from one of the neighboring frats.

I wasn't sure what to do with myself, so I turned around and leaned back against the wall, like it was completely normal to hang around, handcuffed in the entrance of a frat house.

Seth closed the door and grabbed a guy dressed as Chucky.

"You're on candy duty, okay? You get bored, you grab someone else. Billy and I are going Trick or Treating."

He grabbed a bucket shaped like a ghost and thrust it into my hand. He took one for himself, grabbed my arm and dragged me out the door.

CHapTer THree

I was stunned. "What? You're taking me out like this?"

"Of course." Seth adjusted his grip on my arm. "You're my prisoner." I bit my lip — I was enjoying this way too much. His secure grip on my arm was a reassurance in some way, he wasn't going to leave me somewhere. He was still with me. Of course, out on the street, everyone could see my predicament, but they probably wouldn't think anything of it. They'd assume it was a planned Halloween schtick.

Planned.

Like Seth had chosen this costume on purpose, found these cuffs — which by the way — were not the flimsy thin metal cuffs that usually came with costumes like this. These were the real deal, thick shackles that weighed my arms down. The padlock he'd used to secure them to the waist chain was the real thing, too, he'd need to use a key to unlock it. People didn't just have these things lying around, unless they planned to use them, right?

"You planned this, didn't you Seth?"

"Sure. I've seen the way you look at me. The way you annoy me just to get attention. Well, you got it, and I'm going to punish you for not being up front and just talking to me." He tugged on my arm, almost making me stumble. "This is part of it. Walking up around so everyone can see you belong to me. That enough attention for you?"

His words did sinful things to me. I tried to shake free of his grip, just to be rewarded with him yanking me closer against his side. The chains clanked with the movement, and it sounded like music to my ears. I loved everything about this treatment. He'd seen right through me and understood something that even I hadn't. I didn't just want his attention, I wanted him to subjugate me. I wanted to belong to him, to be his, and only his. How had he known?

"How does that make you feel, Billy?"

My mouth went dry. "I dunno."

Seth let go of me to slap my ass smartly with the palm of his hand. The impact spread like heat through my body, and I immediately craved more.

"Answer me, prisoner." He spanked me again.

I yelped. "I like it!" I hadn't meant to give in so quickly, but on the other hand, he already had me tied up. I wanted to see how far Seth would go.

"Good. Thought so. If you behave, I'll take you back to my room, spank you and fuck you until you come so hard you see stars."

I swallowed, that sounded like my best wet dream.

"And if I don't behave?"

Seth took hold of my arm again. "Then I'll still do all of that, but you won't get to orgasm."

I moaned, couldn't help myself. Denial was the cruelest and most arousing thing at the same time.

Seth smirked.

We didn't even visit any of the houses or collect candy. He was just marching me up and down the road, letting everyone see. Some people were taking photos of us. I was glad for the candy pail because it covered the hardness I couldn't control.

I saw people from my classes, girls from our sister sorority, two guys from our frat dresses as pirates, one chasing the other.

Everyone knew I was chained up. They could see it, they knew. It was humiliating but powerful at the same time. I liked people knowing that Seth had done it to me. That Seth wanted me enough to catch me, and chain me up.

My erection was getting a bit unmanageable. The pail masked it somewhat, but the costume did nothing at all to hide it.

I tried to think instead of dull things — the question I had to write about in my next biology assignment. It worked but only a little bit.

"Seth," I said, wheedling. "I uh, I need to go back."

"Call me Sir." But he stopped, looking at me critically. Under his gaze my erection went instantly back to full strength.

"Sir, uh, this bucket can't hide everything."

"I see. Horny young men can't hold it back, can you? Should just fuck you out here, so how good you can be at keeping quiet."

Fuck, why was everything he said doing so much to me? "I'm not good at that," I advised, hurriedly.

"Should have guessed. Big mouth like yours, always poking the bear."

He turned us back towards our frat house.

Relief washed over me and was fast replaced with excited anticipation. I wanted Seth to keep talking, tell me all those dirty things he wanted to do. I had to poke the bear again.

"My mouth is pretty big, I bet I could take you pretty deep in it."

"Another bet?" Seth glanced at me, his grip on my arm tightening. "What are the stakes this time?"

I swallowed. I didn't exactly mean it like a wager, and I didn't want him to make good on his threat of orgasm denial.

"I didn't —"

"You keep taking like that and you'll be on the badly behaved list, Billy."

So, he hadn't forgotten his threat. Maybe he even wanted me to fail so he could do it, have me chained up and begging, unfulfilled. Hot as that image was, I wanted to come.

I kept quiet.

Once we were inside the frat, he lifted me up over his shoulder in a fireman's carry, and climbed the stairs like I weighed nothing. Hot, everything he did was so fucking hot.

In his room he kicked the door shut. Still holding me over his shoulder he spoke. "Before we go any further, I need your safeword and your STI status."

"Free of STIs," I panted. My blood was going to my head, being inverted like this. "I don't need a safeword."

"Cute." Seth spanked me again. "Your safeword can be 'smart Alec', got that?"

I tugged on the manacles again. "Fine."

"Now." He set me down on my feet so I could watch as he removed his hat and sunglasses, "Undress me, Billy."

"But... I can't?" I yanked on the cuffs, anchored to my waist, as if he'd somehow forgotten.

"You were bragging about your mouth, let's see how clever you can be with it."

For once, I didn't have a comeback for that.

"Get started, prisoner, I'm waiting."

Flushed, I moved closer, leaning in to bite the collar of his shirt. Once I had a firm grip, I tugged it off his shoulder, moving behind to yank with my teeth. He helped some, moving his arms as the fabric slipped down.

"That wasn't so hard, was it?" Now, my shorts."

I went to my knees in front of him and examined his shorts. Thankfully these were costume pants, not jeans with a belt, button and fly to contend with. No, these were cheap polyester, closed with Velcro. I leaned in, pressing my nose into his stomach as I carefully gripped the top flap of the fastening.

Once I had a firm grip with my teeth, I shuffled back on my knees to pull the Velcro open. The formally mundane sound of Velcro opening would forever after be an erotic sound to me. As his shorts came open his bulging underwear came out — under the shorts he wore only a jockstrap, and his package was clearly huge. I groaned, desperately wanted to get to him.

I mouthed over the jockstrap, worshiping him, horny and sloppy and not giving a single shit about it. I wet the fabric with my saliva, pleasure shooting through me when I heard his moan of approval.

He fisted a hand in my hair, tugging sharply. "Get my shorts off, pet."

Right, right, I had a job. I nipped at the waistband of his shorts, not being too careful of his skin, and yanked them down.

His hand tightened in my hair again. "Careful where you bite."

I resisted a mad urge to bite his inner thigh, not wanting to be punished. Finally, I'd made enough progress yanking his shorts down that he had to let go of my hair. The shorts were so tight I had to work them slowly down his legs, my jaw beginning to ache.

I was almost groveling at his feet by the time I got them to his ankles.

"Stay down there, Prisoner."

I rested my chin on the floor, breathing heavily from the arousal and the hard work.

He stopped out of the shorts and removed the jock strap himself. I wished he was wearing proper police boots so I could lick them.

I had to lick something. I sat up to lick a stripe up the length of his sizeable cock.

He groaned. "Can I trust you not to bite me, prisoner?"

I nodded. "Yeah."

"Call me Sir, I said. Any time you address me and ask to be given my cock."

I was already bright red, but I felt my cheeks heat even more. I wasn't about to back out or piss him off now.

"Please, Sir, please give me your cock in my mouth?"

He grinned and pushed himself past my lips. "Get me ready to fuck you."

I moaned around him. I'd always loved giving head, and he was large enough to provide a challenge. I leaned in, encouraging him to push further in.

He did so, shoving into my gag reflex and past it. I choked, pulled back and then leaned in to take it again.

Seath caressed my skull with his large fingers. So much strength even in those. I felt so small next to him, smaller kneeling at his feet. It felt right to be sucking him off, while he stood over me.

But I was protected too. I knew he'd be rough with me, but he'd stop if I asked. He'd shove me around, spank me, but he wouldn't truly hurt me. Chained up at his feet, I felt protected.

I worked him over, using all the tricks I knew, until he pulled me off by the hair.

"You want me to fuck you?"

"Yeah, so bad, Sir."

"First I gotta get you into position, just how I want you."

Chapter Four

He pulled me to my feet and stripped the costume pants off me. He turned me around and grabbed a bottle of lube. Before I knew it, he was fingering me open, pushing lube up inside me with rough movements.

I moaned, my knees threatening to buckle at any moment. He spent far too short a time prepping me before slipping a slim, lubed vibrator into me. It wasn't my first time using a sex toy, but I usually spent more time building up to it. I whined as the stretch stung me.

"Just think of it prepping you for me, pet."

I moaned, because it did make it easier to take, and a million times hotter, thinking about what was going to come next.

He yanked on my arm, marching me towards his desk, which was pulled out from the wall and cleared of papers and books. Seth grabbed a set of keys and unlocked the padlock and shackles. I whimpered. I wasn't ready to be untied.

"Don't fuss, prisoner." He stripped off the costume top and tossed it aside. "Bend over the desk and spread your legs."

I did as he said, putting my hands flat on either side of my head. He slapped my ass — the smarting sensation heightened by the jostle to the vibe in my ass. I whined again, needy and pathetic even to my own ears.

Roughly, as if he thought I was in danger of making a break for it, he yanked my arm straight, cuffed me and secured the chain to the leg of the desk. He repeated the action with my other arm so I was chained, spread across his desk with my ass up. He bent down and pushed my legs even further apart.

He snapped a shackle closed around my ankle and tugged it to secure it to the front leg of the desk. I tugged against it as he did the same with my other ankle.

"How many pairs of cuffs do you even have?"

"Enough to keep you secure," he replied.

He stroked a surprisingly gentle hand up my leg, caressing the muscles there.

"Please don't tease me now! I'm so hard."

He spanked me again and I groaned. "How do you address me?"

"Sir, Sir, I'm sorry, please don't tease me."

"What do you want, prisoner?" His hand moved up to tug my balls and I whined.

"Please fuck me Sir, I'm so hard for you, I'm ready for you, please fuck me!"

Seth groaned. "I could hear you begging for me all night long, sounds so good."

I bit my lip, would he really hold out and just keep me on the edge? Part of me wanted that, wanted to know how it would feel to be edged for that long.

"Not tonight though, gotta take advantage while you're tied up like this."

He reached up to tug on the vibrator, not enough to pull it out, just enough to tease me with the motion of it. I groaned, my voice cracking, loud and debauched.

He pulled it out with a swift motion and positioned himself behind me.

"Ready for this?"

"Yes, please! Please fuck me Sir!"

He pushed inside with agonizing slowness, his hand smoothed down my spine, pressing me down gently. It was a gentle motion, but it felt possessive. He was reminding me I was his.

As if I could forget with all these chains pinning me over his desk as he fucked me.

I whined, squirming, wanting more.

His hand pressed harder between my shoulder blades, stilling my movement. "You'll get what you need, pet, just hush for me, be patient."

I whined, panting, I didn't dare speak again. Not when he'd told me to hush. I screwed my eyes shut and breathed out. All at once a peace overcame me.

I wasn't in charge here. What happened next was entirely up to Seth. Seth would take care of me, and that meant, I didn't have to worry or stress or whine. I could relax and be his treasured pet, his prisoner.

It was bliss like I'd never felt before. All my desire to annoy him, to make smart comebacks and jokes was foreign to me, I felt as cozy and safe as if he'd wrapped me in a warm blanket, instead of chains.

"That's it, that's a good boy." He murmured.

He started to rock his hips, pumping in and out of me as I moaned, breathy and high, almost girlish.

He stroked his hand up to the base of my neck and held me there, a secure grip like he had me in a collar. His other hand was on my hip, holding me in place as he shoved inside. I groaned.

My cock was pressed between me and the desk and although the chafing was on the painful side, I was enjoying every second of it. With the urgency of my need subsumed in the floaty feeling of security I simply let it happen. Seth would take care of that, when it was time.

He increased the speed, and I heard his groans and grunts, the way he was enjoying me, and it heightened my own pleasure.

"Want to come for me?"

He tugged my hips up so get access to my dick, the cuffs on my wrists and ankles strained but it didn't hurt, it was a blissful reminder of how bound I was.

"Yes, please Daddy."

Seth stopped moving and I bit my lip. I was supposed to call him Sir, but Daddy had just slipped out... he had such Daddy energy.

I was about to apologize when his grip on the base of my neck tightened.

When he spoke his voice was low and gravely. "Call me that again."

"Daddy?"

He moaned louder, fisted my cock in his hand and started railing me hard and fast. "Fuck that's hot."

I moaned, I was so close to coming but I wasn't sure if I was really allowed to. "Please, Daddy!"

"Come." He slammed himself deep inside, his hips tight against my ass.

I bucked against his hand and came, practically screaming. Probably everyone in the frat house had heard that but in that moment my caring was non-existent. I was Seth's, and I wanted everyone to know it.

He thrust a few more times, his movements shaky and erratic before he pulled out to spill over my ass. I felt the dampness hit my cheeks and up to my lower back. He was marking me.

I moaned again, my voice breaking.

He stroked his hands over my back, used one hand to rub some of his cum into my skin and then pulled out with a sigh.

CHAPTER FIVE

I melted, boneless onto the desk, focusing on catching my breath and nothing else.

I felt a tug at my leg as Seth undid the shackles. He moved around the desk, unlocking me, then he gathered my limp form into his arms and carried me to bed.

He lay down with me draped over his lap.

I was still coming down from an orgasm that seemed to have destroyed my mind.

I focused on breathing in, breathing out and remembering what my name was.

Slowly, I realized he was talking to me. His voice low and soft, soothing.

I made a huge effort and tuned into his words.

"You were so good, such a good sub for me, I'm so proud of you Billy."

I opened my eyes — when had I closed them? — and smiled up at him. "Proud?"

He grinned. "Yeah, proud. Welcome back."

He kissed my nose, making me laugh.

"You were incredible, pet."

I nuzzled in against his muscular chest and sighed happily. "You're incredible."

He hummed and played with my hair, petting me like a dog.

Drink this." He passed me a sports drink and I downed half of it before snuggling into him again. I don't think I'd ever been cuddled like this before, and I liked it.

I wanted to stay like this forever. Fuck, I hoped he didn't mean this to be a one and done, I'd never recover if I never had sex like that again. I had to clear it up immediately or all my good feelings would evaporate.

"Can we do that again?"

He grinned, leaning into kiss the top of my head. "Yes. Any time you like."

"Really? So like, every day of the week and twice on Sundays?"

Seth laughed. "There's that smart mouth of yours, beginning to think I broke you."

I blushed and hid my face in his chest. "Fuck, you saying that turns me on now."

"Good." Seth tugged gently on my hair until I looked up at him. "Yes, as often as we both have energy for, and no missing classes or assignments. But I want to take you as my submissive, you in?"

I nodded; I didn't need to know anything more than that. "Yes, please, Daddy."

He closed his eyes. "That does things to me. Don't abuse it, or I'll punish you for real next time."

I grinned wide and sat up to look him directly in the eye, recalling what I'd said at the start of the night. "Don't threaten me with a good time."

He tackled me.

CHASED

and Bound in Public

A Halloween MM BDSM Erotica

D LaMarque

CHAPTER ONE

Nearly there, so close — The door to my room opened while I was beating off.

Hurriedly, I slammed my laptop closed and yanked my hand out of my pants.

"What the —?" Mal closed the door behind him. "If you're going to self-pleasure, you should really lock the door, Harry."

I tried to recover myself, bright red in the face. This was NOT happening. "Ever heard of knocking before entering?!"

"Sorry, bud." Mal laughed, reached past me and opened the laptop again.

"No!" I was too slow. The same gay BDSM porn I'd been getting off too started playing in the browser window. A red-headed twink was bound and gagged, while a larger guy fucked him relentlessly.

I slammed my hand over the power button, cutting it off. "Mal! What are you doing?"

Mal raised an eyebrow. "That's what you're into, huh?"

"Shut up and please leave me alone." I placed my head on the desk and willed the earth to open up and devour me.

To my surprise, Mal put his hand on my shoulder, a soothing gesture. When he spoke again, the teasing tone had vanished. "It's nothing to be ashamed of Harry. Sorry for freaking you out."

I tensed, couldn't help it. I wasn't sure what to make of the sudden change in his tone. Was he placating me now just so he could go and tell the rest of our frat brothers and have a laugh?

I didn't look at him. "Um, that's nice and all but do you mind leaving while I try to gather up the last vestiges of my dignity?"

Mal laughed. "So dramatic."

I looked up finally. "I am studying English Literature, it's all drama."

Mal squeezed my shoulder and let go. "I was just checking that you're all sorted with a pirate costume? Trick or Treat has started outside and I was about to get changed."

I nodded towards the outfit I'd put together on the bed. Mal and I had agreed on pirates a few days ago and I had found a few suitable things at the local thrift shop: Brown pants, white shirt, brown vest and tall boots — a kind of Will Turner from Pirates of the Caribbean thing. I had shoulder-length hair and the same kind of pointy nose as him so I figured I could pull it off.

"Nice. So, uh..." Mal trailed off.

I turned in my swivel chair and looked up at him. "Dude, why are you still here?"

"Because." He licked his lips. Mal was hot as fuck, tall, muscled and with umber skin that shone. Every time he licked his lips it distracted me. I'd often wondered what it would be like to have his dick in my mouth, but I'd never been brave enough to make any kind of move.

"Listen, Harry, I interrupted you, and I'm sorry. How about I make it up to you?"

My mouth went dry and my mind went blank. Full smooth brain as I tried to comprehend what he could possibly be offering. "What?"

Mal looked deep into my eyes. "You top or bottom?"

My smooth brain didn't understand. "Huh?"

"You watch those videos. When you do, do you want to be the one in charge, or the one in chains?" Mal explained, patiently.

"I..." yes, he had really just asked that, all earnestly like he genuinely wanted to know. "Why?"

"Because I see you watching stuff like that, and it makes me want to tie you to the bed and fuck you 'til you scream. That's all."

My erection came back instantly. "Oh. Bottom. Chains." That was all I could manage to say, hardly eloquently but it got the point across.

Mal grinned wolfishly, gripped my hair with one hand, pulled my head back and kissed me. It was bruisingly intense, and my entire body responded to it.

I moaned into his mouth, surprise and temporary inability to think melting into just one need — to obey Mal.

"Good." Mal let go of my hair, stood up straight and dusted off his pants. "See you in a half hour, we'll hit the candy trail, then we'll see what happens."

He strode out of the room, not even waiting for my reply, and leaving me vaguely dazed, like, had that even happened? Did I dream it somehow?

I tried to process it for a few minutes. I opened my laptop, killed the browser tabs with porn in them and closed it up.

Before I got into my costume, I went to the bathroom with a bottle of lube. I spent about ten minutes teasing myself open, making sure I was prepped and ready for Mal. Whatever was going to happen, I wanted to be ready for it. He'd said tie me up and fuck me, and I hoped he'd meant it.

Was I reading too much into 'we'll see what happens'? Probably. But fuck it. Our frat held an annual Halloween party. If Mal hadn't meant anything really, maybe I could find a one-night-stand… or just play with one of my dildos.

Once I was stretched to three fingers, I washed up and went back to my room to dress in my pirate costume. I ran my hands through my hair and pulled my tall boots on. I decided against shaving since it made me look more rogueish.

I looked in the mirror — I looked fine, passable. Probably should have gotten myself a broad-brimmed hat but it was too late now.

Summoning up my courage I knocked on Mal's door. I was nervous. What was he thinking about? Was he going to kiss me again? Or had it all been a joke? What would he do?

"Come in," he called.

I let myself inside.

Mal was half-dressed, pants on, pulling his shirt on as I closed the door. I took in the view of his chiseled abs, well-muscled abs and the expanse of his perfect olive-toned skin. I wanted him so bad I started to salivate.

"You look good, Harry." He finished dressing and grabbed a black broad-brimmed hat, strapped on a sword and picked up a coil of rough-looking brown rope.

"What's the rope for?"

Mal grinned, his usual wolf-grin, all teeth. It looked positively demonic with the piratical accouterments.

"This? It's for you, Harry. If you want it."

I swallowed, shifting my weight from one foot to the other. My mouth was flooded with so much saliva I had to swallow again.

"So? What do you think? I'm the captain of the pirate ship who took yours, and I took you prisoner as part of the booty?"

I nodded, blushing. "Yeah, I want you — I mean, I want that."

"Good boy." Mal nodded, satisfied. "Now, there's what I'm thinking."

He beckoned me closer and I walked to him as if hypnotized.

"You tell me your safeword, confirm you're STI-free. Then I'll chase you. When I catch you, I'll tie you up and then we grab some candy and come back here."

"You'll tie me up and *then* we get candy?"

Mal grinned. "Sure, it's in theme. Pirates are always tying each other up in the movies."

I took a deep breath, considering. I wanted Mal and the ropes very much.

How did I feel about doing it in public? I knew I should say no, but... the idea was making me a thousand times more horny. It was audacious, scandalous, sinful even, but the thought of Mal chasing me, catching me, tying me up where people could see? It hit all my most secret fantasies.

He was really offering it.

I couldn't say no. I nodded.

"I need enthusiastic consent, puppy."

I swallowed. "Yes, I consent. I'm very, very aroused by your plan. I'm STI free and my safeword is..." I'd never used one before. I used the first word that popped into my head. "Lincoln."

"Good." Mal kissed my cheek, and slipped the coil of rope over his shoulder. "I'll give you a thirty second head start." He lifted his watch — the only thing that looked anachronistic about his costume — and tapped it. "Starting now."

"Thirty seconds, is that all? Are you serious?"

"Oh yeah. Better run, the big bad pirate is coming for you."

CHAPTER TWO

I didn't need to be told twice. I ran — slamming out of his room and down the stairs. Some of the brothers were setting up for the party, creating an obstacle course to navigate. I dodged past them as quickly as I could.

"Careful, dude!"

"Slow Mal down, will you?" I shouted and bolted out the door.

"What? Why?"

Thirty seconds wasn't much time. If he'd given me five minutes, or even ten, it could have been a fairer race. I'd ask for longer next time — assuming there was a next time, of course. Couldn't assume this was anything more than Halloween fun.

I got to the end of the path that led to the Psi Phi Sigma house and hesitated. Should I go left or right? I was losing precious seconds just on indecision. I could hear noise behind me, the frat brothers getting in Mal's way, maybe. I had to move.

I took left on impulse, either way there were places to hide and people to obscure me.

I jogged down the road, looking around for some place to hide.

"Avast! Ye scurvy scoundrel! Get back here!" Mal shouted from behind.

I broke into a run, briefly wondering why I had chosen to wear tall boots. I'd have been a lot faster in my running shoes. But it wouldn't have gone with the costume.

The road was busy — crowds of people in costumes clustering together. I ducked around a crowd of sorority girls dressed as zombie cheerleaders and used their cover to get behind a small group of guys in vampire and werewolf outfits. I glanced back to see Mal looking at the girls, I'd evaded him for the moment.

The challenge of the chase hit me — there was a challenge, a game, and although I wanted to lose. I wanted to be tied up and fucked, and that meant I had to lose. But I wanted to make it hard for Mal. Make him work for it.

Mal jogged past, following the cheerleaders, and I doubled back, turning to run again. I crashed directly into a guy dressed as a swamp monster.

The force of the impact had made him step back and his candy bucket had fallen from his gloved hand.

"Sorry, sorry." I crouched to collect up the spilled candy and hand him his bucket back.

When I straightened up, a hand clamped around my arm.

"Gotcha."

Mal.

I twisted on instinct, pulling out of his grasp. "No, you don't!"

I saw a clear path up the road and sprinted, laughing as Mal swore behind me. He'd put on a Captain Jack Sparrow accent and he sounded absolutely ridiculous.

My feet slapped the pavement as I put distance between myself and my pursuer.

This was easy enough, I was a morning jogger, and Mal's workouts were mostly weights-based, if I remembered right.

How long could I draw this out? How angry would he be if I made him chase me for hours? Did I even want to do that?

Although, I couldn't hear him behind me?

I glanced back over my shoulder — nothing. I couldn't see him, just a bunch of random trick or treaters. I scanned the crowd again, looking for the signature black hat and red bandanna but seeing nothing.

My heart pounded, and not just from the running. I was afraid. It was a bit like being in a horror movie, knowing someone was after me, and I couldn't see them.

But I'd never imagined being so turned on from the feeling of being hunted.

I slowed to a jog, this must be what deer felt like when they were separated from the herd. There was a large tree out front of a sorority house, so I slowed and slunk into the shadows cast by it. They'd hung rubber bats from the branches, and I hoped they'd somehow mask me taking shelter there.

I tried to catch my breath, my blood was singing, all senses on alert for possible sounds of pursuit.

A hand clamped tight over my mouth.

CHAPTER THREE

I cried out, the natural response to being grabbed from behind. Then I felt the cold steel of a knife pressed to my Adam's apple. I froze up.

I knew Mal wouldn't have a real knife, nothing with a dangerous blade on it, but I hadn't known he'd had a knife and the surprise of it was a thrill that went straight to my dick.

"Hands in the air."

I raised my hands in front of me slowly.

"Gotcha this time. Slippery little thing, aren't you? Thought you could escape Captain Mal?"

I mumbled my response against his hand. I could taste the sweat from his palm on my lips. Salty, like he really was a pirate who'd recently been in the ocean spray.

He removed his hand and I immediately wished he hadn't. The feel of his hand on my mouth had been pleasant, I'd felt secure somehow, owned. Hot as Hell.

"Put your hands behind your back. If you scream for help I'll cut you, don't think I won't." he'd abandoned the Jack Sparrow impression and instead spoke in a low, husky version of his own voice. It went right through me.

I put my hands behind my back, crossing the wrists. The knife came away from my throat. It was most likely a butter knife, but I felt a wave of relief even so.

Mal tied my hands with rope, winding it around and then between my crossed wrists, and knotting it tight. He yanked on the ropes, checking their security maybe? I grunted at the strength of the tug, shifting my feet to a more balanced stance so he didn't yank me right over.

My mouth went dry as he wound more rope over my chest, weaving it under and over my upper arms to keep them tight against my torso. It was restrictive in the best way . He knew his stuff. I could feel that I'd barely be able to move my arms when he was done.

A soft moan escaped me, I hoped he wouldn't notice, but he was too close for that.

"Want to just tie you to the trunk of this tree and fuck you like that. Too many people around, right now though."

I moaned louder this time, biting my lip so passers-by wouldn't hear me.

"You like that idea? Maybe we can come back when everyone's asleep. Pretend like it's the mast of my ship and I've just captured you all over again."

I pushed back against him at his words. Grinding my ass against his crotch. I could feel a half-chub there, and I wanted to make it harder.

Apparently it just took a little bit of rope and I became a shameless slut. It felt good.

Mal's hand gripped my right asscheek and squeezed. "Gagging for it aren't you?"

I whimpered, needy, as I nodded.

"Good. Let's gag you for real." He pulled his bandanna from under his hat and wrapped it around my mouth. "Open up."

I opened my mouth, nothing in me wanted to resist him now. My cock was hard against the pants I'd chosen and I wanted more.

He tied the fabric tight, so I couldn't quite close my teeth over it.

Mal moved in front of me, taking me in with hungry eyes. "If you want to stop, or slowdown, kick my ankle, got it?"

I nodded, knowing there was no way I would do anything to stop him. I'd never been so turned on. Never in my wildest dreams had I imagined such a night.

He tied another piece of rope to the loops on my chest and knotted it, leaned in and kissed me over the cleave gag. I moaned into it.

I wished he'd been able to tie me to the tree like he'd said, imagining the solid trunk at my back, the ropes holding me to it. I hoped he'd meant it when he said we might come back.

He yanked on the last piece of rope, using it like a leash to bring me with him as he turned and walked out from under the relative shelter of the tree.

Fuck.

This was really happening. He was walking me through the crowded street tied up. People were filming us, snapping photos, calling out.

"Captain Sparrow's caught Will Turner!" Someone yelled.

"What're you going to do, roger the cabin boy?"

"Hot guys, very hot!"

The attention made my cheeks burn but I kind of loved it at the same time. It made me feel special somehow. Wanted. Mal could have anyone he liked — girl, boy, genderqueer or anything — he was cute, popular, smart… but he'd chosen me to tie up. He'd taken *me* prisoner. Heck, he'd suggested the pirates costumes even before he'd walked in on my porn-watching.

I watched his back as he led me on a rope, besotted.

He didn't waste any time now he'd caught me. He led the way straight back to the frat house. The party was filling up, and Mal stopped in the entrance to the living area.

"Here ye! Here ye!" he shouted. Everyone turned to look at us. "I have captured Harry. He's mine. His booty belongs to Captain Mal. Hands off all of you, or I'll make you walk the plank!"

My face was on fire, but I loved what he was saying.

His announcement was met with hoots and cheers.

"Finally!"

"Have fun, Harry!"

"Good work, Captain Mal!"

"Yeah, have fun!"

"I intend to." Mal yanked me up the stairs by the rope leash.

CHAPTER FOUR

Mal shoved me into his room so hard I stumbled, almost tripping over my own boots.

"Now, to get you ready..." He crouched and took hold of my boot, helping me to remove them. I lifted my foot and balanced carefully as he took care of them.

"Good prisoner, so cooperative. You want me to call you Cabin Boy? I kind of liked the sound of that."

I shook my head, I liked the way he'd talked about capturing me, making me his prisoner.

He yanked my pants down and manhandled me over the bed with my ass in the air. He undid the gag and I spat it out.

"I like prisoner," I said the second I could. "Or Captive, Sir." I got a thrill from calling him Sir like the subs did in the pornos I watched.

"Call me Captain." He slapped my ass.

"Sorry, Captain. I'm your prisoner, I like to hear you call me that."

Mal hummed his approval and slapped my other ass-cheek. The he spread them open and teased at my hole.

"What's this? Did you get ready for me? Or did you prep yourself just for anyone? How much of a whore are you, prisoner?"

"It's for you, Captain." I groaned. It was close to the truth, I'd hoped it would be him when I stretched myself.

He pushed his finger in to the knuckle and stroked my prostate with his fingertip. I squirmed, loving the sensation but partially wanting to escape the direct pressure as well.

"You didn't know I'd catch you. I think you're a no-good, wanton doxy, ready to give it up to anyone. Just a boy for sale, is that it?"

Fuck, why did he make that sound so hot?

I groaned, turned on as much by his words as his actions.

"But whatever, you're mine now, and you've saved me some time."

He withdrew his finger and pushed my head down with his other hand. "Any last words before I ravish you, captive?"

I swallowed, I was ready for him, but he'd removed the gag and I missed it. "Gag me, please Captain."

Mal moaned, my words had aroused him. "Fuck, such a whore for me. I'll give you what you want, prisoner."

He grabbed the bandanna, which was already wet from my saliva, and pressed it into my mouth so it was behind my teeth.

Then he wound another length of rope around my head, pressing it between and over my lips and tying it at the back of my skull. I could feel the roughness of the rope, pressing into my cheeks and holding the bandanna in place.

He wound the rope around my neck next, making a makeshift collar that pressed firmly on my throat. I almost came on the spot, but I held it back with a huge effort.

"Gonna keep you." His voice was a low growl of a promise.

He spread my cheeks and pressed into me, I'd lost track of when he'd stripped off his own pants, too wrapped up in the ropes and the sensations of wanting. He moved slowly, allowing me to stretch around him.

I moaned his name, the sound so muffled by the gag that it came out as nonsense.

He slipped his fingers between my arm and my bonds to grip the ropes. He used them as leverage as he buried himself deep inside.

"Mmmm!" I tried to beg him to move faster, but again it came out as nothing but noises.

"Fuck, you're so tight Harry, my prisoner."

He started to pump his hips, tugging on the ropes with every thrust. The ropes pressed hard against me, if I hadn't still been wearing my shirt I'm sure I'd have rope burns. Perhaps I would anyhow? The idea thrilled me.

The ropes were so tight, I tried to struggle, to move my arms, but the ropes constricted all but the smallest of movements. I was more alive in that moment than I'd felt all year. All those videos I'd watched, the daydreams I'd entertained, none of it held a candle to the real experience of being bound up and dominated.

I was stuffed at both ends, Mal filling me with his large cock, and the fabric and rope filling my mouth. I was whole, complete, wanted and used and loving it.

Mal wasn't touching my dick, he was just fucking me, using me for his own gratification. I never wanted the moment to end.

Chapter Five

Mal reached under my hips to stroke my cock. Desperation flooded me.

I wanted to come so much it ached. I'd been so distracted with the chase, the game of it, the roleplaying, and relishing the fantasy come true that I'd put my physical needs to the side.

Now the physical was all I could focus on. I hadn't come, hours ago, watching that video. I hadn't come when he'd tied me up or when he'd filled me, but now. Now I needed it.

"Mm!" I begged, my tongue pressed uselessly against the now-sodden cloth of the gag.

"Hold it." Mal ordered. "You come when I order you to and not a second before, prisoner."

I nodded my head.

"Maybe I shouldn't let you come. Since you're such a whore you prepped yourself, just waiting for someone to come and fill your hole."

I shook my head, suddenly fearful that he wouldn't give permission, or that if I did come anyway, he'd punish me.

He adjusted the angle of his thrusts, pulling me tight against him, and hitting my sweet spot with each pump of his hips.

It was agony, delicious, sensual agony. My every nerve was alive to sensation, all my body responding to the rough treatment and his callous way of speaking to me. *I need it! I need you!* I cried out in my head, hoping somehow he'd know.

He yanked on the ropes again, reminding me I was bound, that I belonged to him. That there was nothing I could do but take it.

I closed my eyes and let myself feel all of it. The gag, ropes cutting into the corners of my mouth, the fabric wadded, threatening to press on my gag reflex. The rope around my neck, tight, the danger of it. The ropes encircling my torso, holding my arms strictly. My position, bent over the bed to take Mal's cock. His hand on my cock, pumping hard, and yet somehow, not enough to actually orgasm, not without his permission.

I lost myself in the overwhelming joy of belonging to Mal.

He groaned, his hips beginning to stutter as he got close. "Come for me, baby." He growled, his voice cracking with need.

I groaned into the gag, my own hips bucking into his hand as I came. It was easy once I had permission.

I spent myself over the bed and whimpered, going limp all over.

Mal's orgasm chased mine, and I felt him filling me, pulling out so some of his seed spilled over my ass.

He pulled all the way out and slapped my ass again. "Fuck that was good."

He moved away, and I wondered if he was going to leave me like this. I didn't want him to go, but my imagination also liked the idea of being left, bound, gagged and fucked out on his bed for him to use later on.

In a moment, Mal was back, gently cleaning me up with a damp cloth. Then he pulled me upright, further up onto the bed, and braced me up while he untied the ropes around my neck and mouth. I opened my mouth as wide as I could so he could tug the fabric out. Something in the movement triggered my gag reflex and I coughed.

"There, that's all right, you're okay, my good boy." Mal's voice was soft, familiar, as he stroked my cheek. "I'm so proud of you, you're a star, Harry."

I licked my lips, shifting my weight a little. I was still bound, but I wasn't about to prompt him to untie me, I liked the feeling of it too much for that.

"You're an incredible dom," I said. My voice was rough, strained from crying out into the gag. "Really, amazing."

Mal kissed me gently and nuzzled my cheek. I hadn't expected such a tender action after all the violence of earlier, but I loved it, loved the way he was handling me as if I was precious, delicate. "Thank you, prisoner."

I nuzzled him back then gently nipped his earlobe. "Like being your prisoner."

"I can tell. That's why I'm not letting you go."

I shivered, happiness flooding me as well as a healthy dose of arousal. "Yeah?"

"Mmhm, gonna keep you. You're going to be a whore just for me, now, Harry. Got it? My submissive and only mine, and I'll try and think of something even more fun to do tomorrow."

I pressed myself further into his arms and he held me tight. "Tie me to the tree, maybe?"

"You like that idea, huh? Being out in public bound?"

I nodded. "It was super hot."

"Then I'll make it happen for you." Mal kissed me again, passionate, a promise. He lay back against the headboard, pulling me between his legs to rest against his chest. "Now, let's watch a movie, until I decide it's time for round two. Sound good?"

He opened his laptop and brought up the first Pirates of the Caribbean movie. I grinned, leaning my head back on his shoulder, tugging against the ropes just a little, to remind myself I was still tied up.

"Sounds absolutely perfect."

ALSO BY

If you enjoyed this please check out my long-form MM(+) spicy, kinky paranormal novels for more:

Cabin Boy (4 book series, Harem/MMMMM)

Kidnapped by the Gentleman (4 book series, harem/MMMM)

Misselthwaite College (duology, MMMM)

Dark Attraction (2 books out, paranormal, human/vampire MM)

Night's Melody (MMMM)

The End of the World (MM, paranormal, portal fantasy)

Other Shorts:

Club K series (contemporary, MM standalones)

Blood for Hire (MM Paranormal, one couple over five nights)

Bunny (Hybrid rabbit, MM, trans lead character)